UP THE CREEK

The Roaring River Run is on! This year the paddlers can pick up points as they make their way upriver. Add the points in each lane to find out who racks up the highest score.

Illustration: Scott Peck

7

1

4

0

1

9

3

0

5

2

6

6

4

3

7

9

8

5

8

4

3

7

2

1

2

2

Answer on page 48

MORE, PLEASE

Answer on page 48

Every summer, the Moores throw a big family party. Choose the correct response in each set of statements.

If there are more children than adults, letter two is H. If not, letter one is C.

If more people are wearing hats, letter four is L. If more people are not wearing hats, letter seven is I.

If there are more people by the grill than by the table, letter six is S. If there are more people near the table, letter six is R.

If there are more dogs than cats, letter one is T. If there are more cats, letter two is A.

If there are more butterflies than birds, letter seven is N. If there are more birds, letter five is O.

If more people have red shirts on than any other color, letter four is M. If more people are wearing blue shirts, letter three is T.

If more people are wearing glasses than not, letter three is E. If more people are not wearing glasses, letter five is I.

Illustration: Jerry Zimmerman

Write the correct letters in the spaces at the bottom of the page to learn the motto of the Moore family.

$\overline{1}$ $\overline{2}$ $\overline{3}$ $\overline{4}$ $\overline{5}$ $\overline{5}$ $\overline{6}$ $\overline{3}$ ' $\overline{1}$ $\overline{2}$ $\overline{3}$ $\overline{4}$ $\overline{3}$ $\overline{6}$ $\overline{6}$ $\overline{7}$ $\overline{3}$ $\overline{6}$

GAME TRACKER

The names of six animals are scattered in the grid below. The first letters of all the names are in red. Once you've figured out which letter starts which word, make the moves given below the other blanks to spell out each word. You will use each letter in the grid only once, and all the letters will be used.

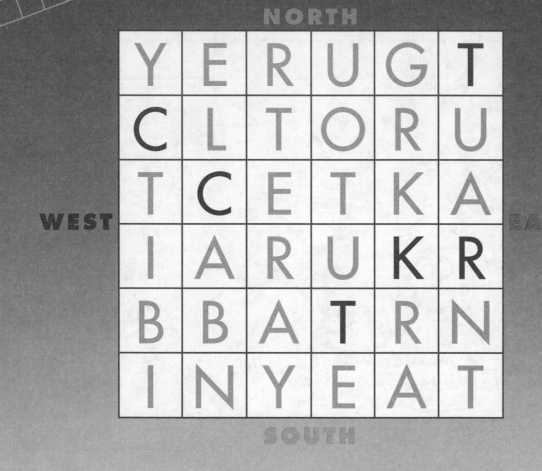

NORTH

Y	E	R	U	G	T
C	L	T	O	R	U
T	C	E	T	K	A
I	A	R	U	K	R
B	B	A	T	R	N
I	N	Y	E	A	T

WEST   **EAST**

SOUTH

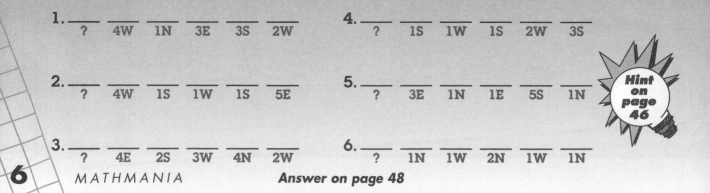

1. ___ ___ ___ ___ ___ ___
   ?   4W   1N   3E   3S   2W

4. ___ ___ ___ ___ ___ ___
   ?   1S   1W   1S   2W   3S

2. ___ ___ ___ ___ ___ ___
   ?   4W   1S   1W   1S   5E

5. ___ ___ ___ ___ ___ ___
   ?   3E   1N   1E   5S   1N

3. ___ ___ ___ ___ ___ ___
   ?   4E   2S   3W   4N   2W

6. ___ ___ ___ ___ ___ ___
   ?   1N   1W   2N   1W   1N

Hint on page 46

6   *MATHMANIA*   **Answer on page 48**

SIMPLE INSTRUCTIONS

Number these shapes in order from simplest to most complex. Once you have them in order, read the letters beneath them, the top line from left to right and then the bottom line, to find the answer to the riddle.

A
S

G
D

N
D

I
I

H
E

Y
!

O
(space)

W
R

H
V

(space)
I

Where do road crews do most of their math work?

Answer on page 48

FLOATING FUN

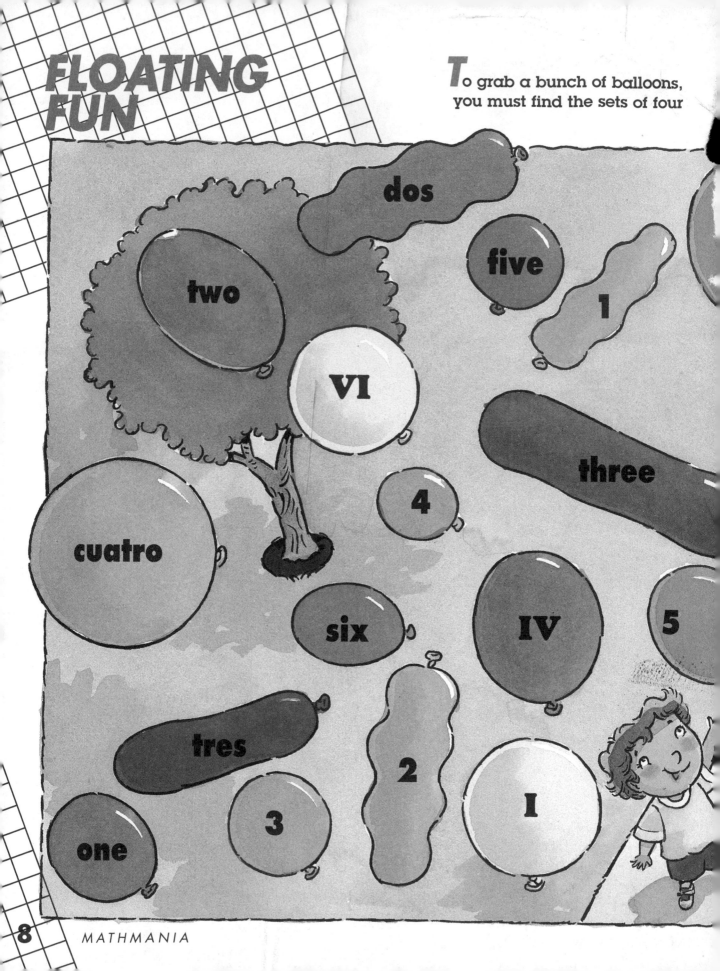

balloons that go together. There are six different sets in all.

Illustration: John Nez

Hint on page 46

Answer on page 48

9

TEN BY TEN

Each clue below can be answered by a word that contains the letters *T-E-N*. We'll TENd to think of you as a puzzle genius once you've writTEN in the answers.

1. Temporary shelter for campers: ___ ___ ___ ___

2. Nervous, on edge: ___ ___ ___ ___

3. Voice range above bass: ___ ___ ___ ___

4. Game with a net and racquets: ___ ___ ___ ___ ___ ___

5. Hear, attend: ___ ___ ___ ___ ___ ___

6. Person who occupies a rental property: ___ ___ ___ ___ ___ ___

7. A guide with a cut-out pattern for painting or printing:

___ ___ ___ ___ ___ ___ ___

8. One octopus arm: ___ ___ ___ ___ ___ ___ ___ ___

9. What you should pay when someone is speaking:

___ ___ ___ ___ ___ ___ ___ ___ ___

10. Nashville is the capital of this state:

___ ___ ___ ___ ___ ___ ___ ___ ___

Answer on page 48

LOST IN THE WOODS

X marks the spot where you are standing in the center of this forest. There are a lot of pathways that lead out along only even-numbered squares. But there is only one path that leads to the edge along odd-numbered squares. Can you find the one path? You may move up, down, left, right, or diagonally.

3	2	4	2	9	4	4	8	5
2	8	1	2	8	6	7	6	4
6	5	6	4	6	1	2	9	6
6	1	3	5	8	3	2	1	8
4	9	8	5	X	4	8	7	6
8	2	7	9	8	6	9	2	6
5	2	2	1	6	8	4	7	4
1	4	3	9	2	6	2	5	4
7	6	2	2	2	6	9	8	6	3

Answer on page 49.

SCRAMBLED PICTURE

Copy these mixed-up rectangles into the spaces on the next page. The letters and numbers tell

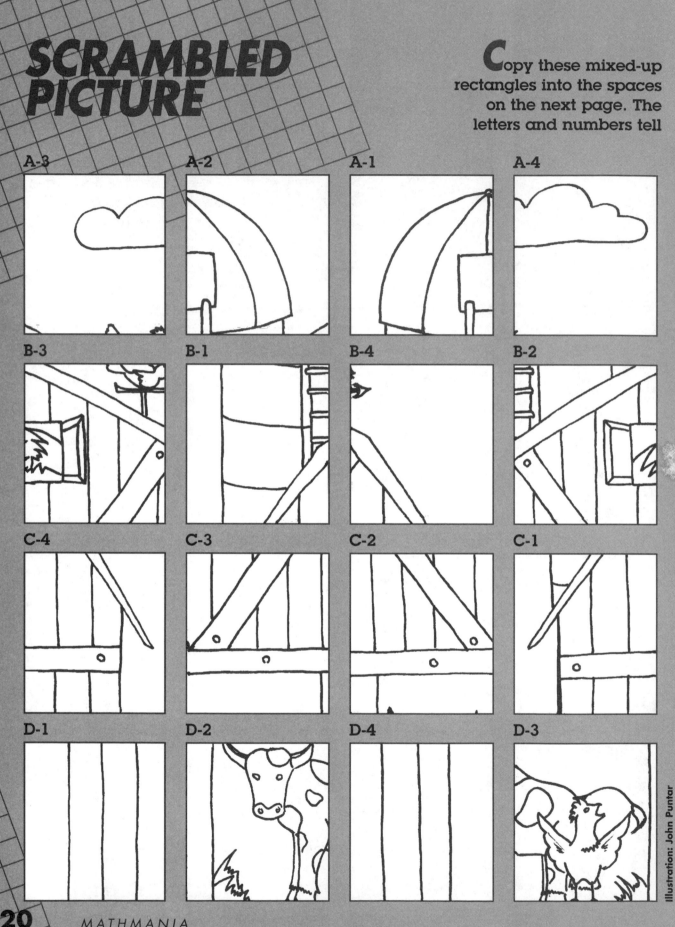

A-3   A-2   A-1   A-4

B-3   B-1   B-4   B-2

C-4   C-3   C-2   C-1

D-1   D-2   D-4   D-3

Illustration: John Puntar

you where each piece
belongs. The first one, A-3,
has been done for you.

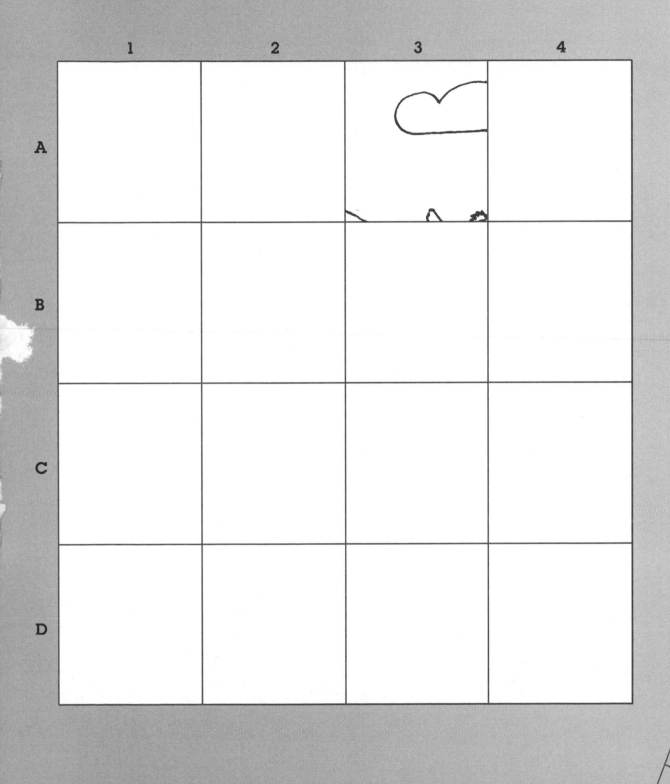

DIGIT DOES IT

Illustration: John Nez

Answer on page 49

for the home team. The angry thief left a coded clue. Help the inspector decipher it.

$\overline{1}\ \overline{10}\ \overline{3}\ \overline{4}$ $\overline{5}\ \overline{6}\ \overline{7}\ \overline{8}\ \overline{10}\ \overline{9}\ \overline{2}\ \overline{11}\ \overline{4}$ $\overline{1}\ \overline{5}\ \overline{12}\ \overline{5}\ \overline{2}$,
$\overline{5}$ $\overline{13}\ \overline{3}\ \overline{14}$ $\overline{15}\ \overline{3}\ \overline{16}\ \overline{10}$ $\overline{1}\ \overline{4}\ \overline{11}\ \overline{8}\ \overline{8}\ \overline{10}\ \overline{1}$ $\overline{2}\ \overline{15}\ \overline{10}$
$\overline{15}\ \overline{11}\ \overline{8}\ \overline{10}\ \overline{17}\ \overline{10}\ \overline{7}\ \overline{7}$ $\overline{1}\ \overline{5}\ \overline{3}\ \overline{13}\ \overline{11}\ \overline{6}\ \overline{1}\ \overline{7}$ $\overline{3}\ \overline{6}\ \overline{1}$
$\overline{7}\ \overline{2}\ \overline{4}\ \overline{18}\ \overline{9}\ \overline{19}$ $\overline{11}\ \overline{18}\ \overline{2}$, $\overline{20}\ \overline{18}\ \overline{2}$ $\overline{14}\ \overline{11}\ \overline{18}$ $\overline{22}\ \overline{5}\ \overline{17}\ \overline{17}$
$\overline{6}\ \overline{10}\ \overline{16}\ \overline{10}\ \overline{4}$ $\overline{2}\ \overline{3}\ \overline{12}$ $\overline{13}\ \overline{10}$ $\overline{20}\ \overline{10}\ \overline{21}\ \overline{11}\ \overline{4}\ \overline{10}$ $\overline{5}$
$\overline{4}\ \overline{10}\ \overline{3}\ \overline{9}\ \overline{15}$ $\overline{15}\ \overline{11}\ \overline{13}\ \overline{10}$. $\overline{5}\ \overline{21}$ $\overline{14}\ \overline{11}\ \overline{18}$ $\overline{1}\ \overline{11}\ \overline{6}\ \overline{2}$,
$\overline{2}\ \overline{3}\ \overline{19}\ \overline{10}$ $\overline{3}\ \overline{6}\ \overline{14}$ $\overline{7}\ \overline{15}\ \overline{11}\ \overline{4}\ \overline{2}$ $\overline{7}\ \overline{2}\ \overline{11}\ \overline{8}\ \overline{7}$,
$\overline{14}\ \overline{11}\ \overline{18}$ $\overline{13}\ \overline{3}\ \overline{14}$ $\overline{21}\ \overline{5}\ \overline{6}\ \overline{1}$ $\overline{2}\ \overline{22}\ \overline{10}\ \overline{6}\ \overline{2}\ \overline{14}$
$\overline{1}\ \overline{5}\ \overline{3}\ \overline{13}\ \overline{11}\ \overline{6}\ \overline{1}\ \overline{7}$ $\overline{20}\ \overline{10}\ \overline{21}\ \overline{11}\ \overline{4}\ \overline{10}$ $\overline{5}$ $\overline{13}\ \overline{3}\ \overline{19}\ \overline{10}$
$\overline{13}\ \overline{14}$ $\overline{22}\ \overline{3}\ \overline{14}$ $\overline{2}\ \overline{11}$ $\overline{2}\ \overline{15}\ \overline{10}$ $\overline{6}\ \overline{10}\ \overline{23}\ \overline{2}$ $\overline{7}\ \overline{3}\ \overline{21}\ \overline{10}$!
$\overline{4}$. $\overline{20}$. $\overline{5}\ \overline{16}\ \overline{10}\ \overline{7}$

Hint on page 46

HIDE AND GO SEEK

Mabel, Maureen, Megan, and Marty are all looking for their pet rabbit, Harvey, who is hiding at one of the numbered intersections. Somehow no one can see Harvey. At which intersection must he be hiding?

7
9
3
2
11
8
1
10
4
6
5

Answer on page 49

NUMBER RECALL

*T*ake 60 seconds to look at the numbers on this page. Try to remember everything here. Then turn the page. Try to answer the questions about these numbers without looking back.

Illustration: Paul Richer

11   7   18

8   2   16

6   14

9

13   12   17

3   4   20

19   15

10   1   5

TIME OUT

How many mistakes can you find on this clock?

Illustration: Paul Richer

NUMBER RECALL PART 2

*T*hese questions are all about the numbers you just saw on page 25. Try to answer them without looking back.

1. Which number is the biggest?
2. Which number is in a circle?
3. Which number has polka dots?
4. Which number is plaid?
5. Which number is on its side?
6. Which number has a shadow?
7. Which number is three-dimensional?
8. Which number is white?

Answer on page 49

SHAPE SHIFTER

Can you fit these five shapes together to form a square?

Hint on page 46

SAND ART

Illustration: Barbara Gray

PLAYING FOR POINTS

Kim scored half as many points as Chad.

Frank and Carol each scored the same number of points.

Bill had three more points than Kim.

Frank had one more point than Kim.

Bill had eight points.

Chad, Kim, Frank, Carol, and Bill were playing a game. Bill was keeping score, but the dog came in and ran off with the scorepad. Can you help figure out the total number of points scored in this game so far, as well as how many points each player had?

Hint on page 47

Answer on page 50

len and Glenda just finished building this model railway system. The layout

TRAINYARD TOUGHIE:
The train, which is a yard long, is traveling at 180 feet per minute as it enters the tunnel. How long does it take for the train to pass completely out to the other end of the tunnel?

A
If each car on the train is six inches long, how many cars make up the train?

features a yard-long
tunnel. The train is also
a yard long.

B

If it takes the train four
minutes to make one
complete circuit of the
track while at its top speed
of 180 feet per minute, how
long is the track?

C

If the train makes the circuit
in six minutes, how fast is it
traveling?

D

If the scale of the track is
1:76, how long would the
real track be?

Hint
on
page
47

E

At that same scale, how
long would the engine be?

Illustration: Jerry Zimmermann

Answer on page 50

MATHMAGIC

Prepare to be astounded by this birthday baffler.

Have a stranger write down the numbers of the month and day she was born.

For instance, Oct. 21 would be 1021. Be sure not to look as she writes the information.

Have her multiply this number by 2 and then add 5.

Multiply this new number by 50.

Now you ask her what number she has come up with. Study the number.

Concentrate. And then, no matter what number she gives you, you'll be able to tell her birthday.

Illustration: Marc Nadel

Answer on page 50

COLOR BY NUMBERS

Color Key
1 — Green   3 — Red   5 — Brown
2 — Blue   4 — Yellow   6 — Black

Illustration: Rob Sepanak

MYSTERIOUS MAP

DIRECTIONS:

All directions begin from START.

1 block = $\frac{1}{4}$ mile

TED
Go east five blocks.
Go north five blocks.
Go west three blocks.

ED
Go north 1 mile.
Go east $\frac{3}{4}$ mile.
Go north $\frac{1}{2}$ mile.
Go east $\frac{1}{4}$ mile.

FRED
Go east until you reach Tamarack Street.
Go north to Third Street.
Turn right and go east to Cherry Street.
Turn left and go north to Fifth Street.
Turn left and go half a block.

JED
Go north to the Donut Shop.
Turn right and drive to Mom's Restaurant.
Then go south to the Fit & Run Shop.
Go east one block.

Hint on page 47

MAX'S GROCERY

ART SUPPLIES

CREATIVE CRAFTS

DONUT SHOP

MAPLE ST.

OAK ST.

LAKESIDE LAWN CARE

ICE CREAM DELIGHTS

START

some spot in Sycamore City. Can you follow the directions to find out where each Berry brother will finish?

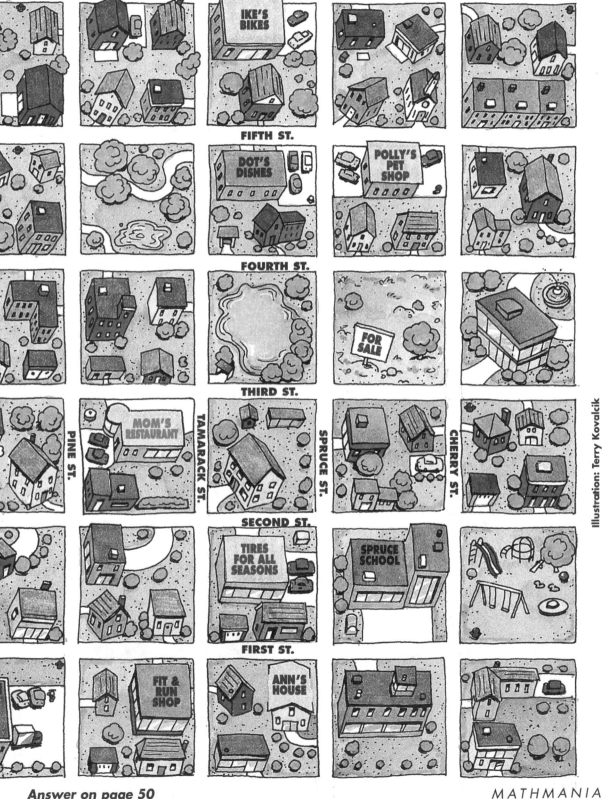

FISH STICKS

These eight sticks and a dime have been made into a fish. Is it possible to move just three sticks and the dime in order to make the fish swim in the opposite direction?

Illustration: Lindy Burnett

Hint on page 47

Answer on page 50

BOAT BUILDER

Can you tell which boat was built from this collection of tubes and boxes?

Illustration: Jim Paillot

A

B

D

C

Hint on page 47

Answer on page 50

WATER WEEK!

Wally Wattle is trying to figure out how much water

ON EACH DAY:

Wendy Wattle takes 1 bath.

Wally takes a shower that lasts 5 minutes.

Willy Wattle takes a shower for 8 minutes.

Wilma Wattle takes 1 bath.

The family flushes the toilet 20 times.

Each of the four members of the family drinks 8 glasses of water each day.

The Wattles do 1 load in the dishwasher each day.

ALSO: The Wattles use the washer 5 times a week.

If Wally is figuring for a seven-day week, how much water did the Wattles use?

Hint on page 47

Each flush of the toilet uses 7 gallons

the Wattle family uses in
a week. Can you help him?

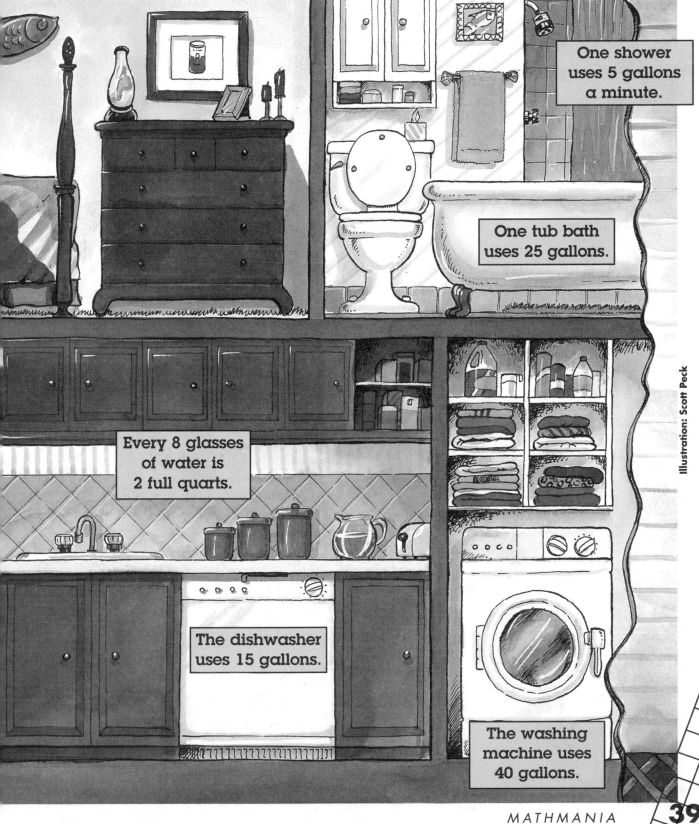

One shower
uses 5 gallons
a minute.

One tub bath
uses 25 gallons.

Every 8 glasses
of water is
2 full quarts.

The dishwasher
uses 15 gallons.

The washing
machine uses
40 gallons.

Illustration: Scott Peck

HOW DOES YOUR GARDEN GROW?

Mary, Mary, quite contrary, planted this garden below. With veggies and flowers, but with the late hour, she's forgotten what went in each row. Use each clue, there are only a few, to figure what's planted where—and then we'll all know.

1. Mary remembers that she alternated rows of vegetables and flowers.
2. She did not plant anything whose name begins with the letter "P" at either end.
3. Mary counted her rows from left to right. Cucumbers are in row 3, next to the primroses.
4. Cabbage is planted between the primroses and the petunias.
5. Besides the items mentioned above, Mary also planted radishes, daisies, pumpkins, and poppies.

Illustration: R. Michael Palan

Answer on page 51

THE BIG L

Can you mark this L shape into four separate shapes, all of the same size and design?

Hint on page 47

FOR THE GREATER GOOD

Answer on page 51

Rachel and Ramon are having a disagreement over who is the greatest—at numbers. Each made a list of fractions. When they

$\frac{1}{2}$

$\frac{1}{8}$

RULES

1. Compare Rachel's list to Ramon's.

2. Award one point to whoever has written the greater number. This means whoever has written the greater fraction gets the point.

Remember, though ¼ looks larger than ½, because the 4 is bigger than the 2, ½ is actually the greater fraction because it is half of something as opposed to just a quarter of something.

3. If the two numbers are equal, neither one gets a point.

$\frac{1}{4}$

$\frac{1}{16}$

A. $\frac{9}{12}$

B. $\frac{3}{4}$

C. $\frac{7}{8}$

D. $\frac{1}{4}$

E. $\frac{4}{5}$

F. $\frac{3}{4}$

G. $\frac{1}{5}$

H. $\frac{7}{8}$

I. $\frac{2}{3}$

J. $\frac{3}{12}$

K. $\frac{4}{12}$

L. $\frac{5}{10}$

compared the two lists, it was hard to tell who had written the greater numbers. Can you help them figure out who scored the most points?

$\frac{1}{12}$

$\frac{1}{6}$

RACHEL **RAMON**

A. $\frac{5}{12}$ A. _____ _____

B. $\frac{9}{12}$ B. _____ _____

C. $\frac{5}{9}$ C. _____ _____

D. $\frac{1}{2}$ D. _____ _____

E. $\frac{5}{6}$ E. _____ _____

F. $\frac{2}{3}$ F. _____ _____

G. $\frac{2}{10}$ G. _____ _____

H. $\frac{1}{2}$ H. _____ _____

I. $\frac{7}{10}$ I. _____ _____

J. $\frac{1}{3}$ J. _____ _____

K. $\frac{1}{3}$ K. _____ _____

L. $\frac{3}{4}$ L. _____ _____

$\frac{1}{3}$

Hint on page 47

Illustration: Paul Richer

MATHMANIA

DEAR LIZA, DEAR LIZA'

This bucket has a hole in it. If you use the scoop, you will pour in two cups' worth of water. But in the time it takes to get the next scoop, a half cup will drip out the hole. The bucket can hold twelve cups of water. How many scoops will it take to fill the bucket, forgetting about any drips from the last scoop?

Hint on page 47

Illustration: Jerry Zimmermann

GRID GRAPPLER

Can you place the numbers 1 through 8 in these boxes, one number per box, so that no two consecutive numbers will be in boxes that touch, whether horizontally, vertically, or diagonally?

Hint
on
page
47

HINTS AND BRIGHT IDEAS

*T*hese hints will help with some of the trickier puzzles.

GAME TRACKER (page 6)
The first answer begins at K. To figure out the other starting letters, look for the ones that allow you to make the moves requested on the rest of that line. You may need to make two or three moves to see if you're spelling out an animal's name.

FLOATING FUN (pages 8-9)
Each set should contain a written number, the numeral for that number, the number in Spanish, and the Roman numeral for that number.

MINUS MALL (pages 12-13)
Look around the mall to find out how much each item costs.

WEIGHT AND WONDER (pages 16-17)
The aliens are trying to load the items from lightest to heaviest. An egg is probably the lightest item on the conveyor belt. What comes next?

VALUABLE INTRODUCTIONS (page 18)
Try to figure out the numerical prefix for each answer. Prefixes are such things as QUADruped (which means a four-footed creature) or HEXAgon (which is a six-sided shape).

DIGIT DOES IT (pages 22-23)
The word *INSPECTOR* appears in the greeting. Use the coded numbers in this word to find the same letters throughout the note.

SHAPE SHIFTER (page 27)
Copy the shapes onto graph paper and cut them out. Then you can rearrange the shapes like a jigsaw puzzle until you make a square.

PLAYING FOR POINTS (page 29)

Though Bill's clue comes last, it might be best to start there and work your way back.

TRAINING GROUND (pages 30-31)

A scale of 1:76 means that every 1 inch (or one foot or one mile) of model track equals 76 inches (or feet or miles) of real track.

MYSTERIOUS MAP (pages 34-35)

Use the key to determine the number of blocks for some directions. The four destinations are Max's Grocery, Ike's Bikes, Polly's Pet Shop, and Ann's House. Now can you figure out who ended up where?

FISH STICKS (page 36)

It may help you figure this one out if you set up the fish with eight toothpicks and a dime.

BOAT BUILDER (page 37)

Make sure the boat you choose uses all the parts shown and that it doesn't have any extra pieces.

WATER WEEK! (pages 38-39)

Remember that Wally is trying to figure out the water usage for a full week. So he may need to multiply some numbers by seven (days in a week) to find his answer. There are four quarts in a gallon.

THE BIG L (page 41)

All four of your shapes will be L's. They will look like the original L, though smaller. Remember: each of your four L's will be the same size.

FOR THE GREATER GOOD (pages 42-43)

Use the circles to help you figure out who has written the greater fraction.

DEAR LIZA, DEAR LIZA (page 44)

Each scoop leaves only a cup and a half of water in the bucket.

GRID GRAPPLER (page 45)

The numbers in the two end boxes are 7 and 2. Consecutive means the numbers that come next to one another. Therefore, neither 1 nor 3 can be in the boxes that touch 2.

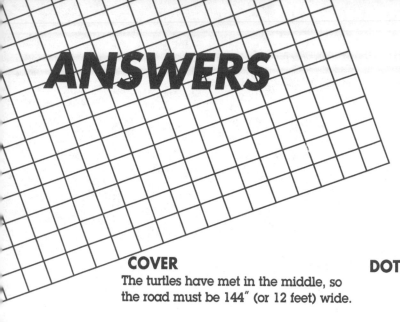

ANSWERS

COVER
The turtles have met in the middle, so the road must be 144" (or 12 feet) wide.

UP THE CREEK (page 3)
From left to right, the totals are:
Lane 1 — 3 + 5 + 9 + 1 + 7 = 25
Lane 2 — 8 + 7 + 2 + 3 + 1 = 21
Lane 3 — 7 + 9 + 6 + 0 + 4 = 26
Lane 4 — 2 + 4 + 8 + 6 + 0 = 20
Lane 5 — 2 + 1 + 3 + 5 + 4 = 15

Lane 3 is the winner.

MORE, PLEASE (pages 4-5)
THE MOORE, THE MERRIER

GAME TRACKER (page 6)
1. kitten
2. rabbit
3. canary
4. turkey
5. cougar
6. turtle

SIMPLE INSTRUCTIONS (page 7)
Where do road crews do most of their math work?

O	N		H	I	G	H	W	A	Y
D	I	V	I	D	E	R	S	!	

FLOATING FUN (pages 8-9)

NUMBER	NUMERAL	SPANISH	ROMAN NUMERAL
one	1	uno	I
two	2	dos	II
three	3	tres	III
four	4	cuatro	IV
five	5	cinco	V
six	6	seis	VI

TEN BY TEN (page 10)
1. tent
2. tense
3. tenor
4. tennis
5. listen
6. tenant
7. stencil
8. tentacle
9. attention
10. Tennessee

DOTS A LOT (page 11)

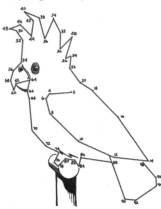

MINUS MALL (pages 12-13)
Florence Finnegan still has $1.00 left.

TRIPLE PLAY (page 14)

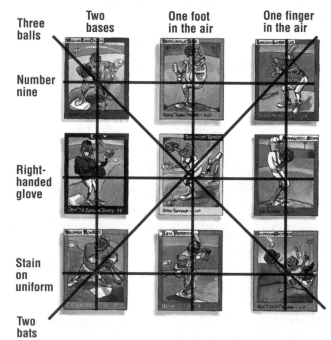

MULTIPLY MOUNTAIN (page 15)

WEIGHT AND WONDER (pages 16-17)
From lightest to heaviest, the items are:
1. egg
2. ice-cream sundae
3. brick
4. pumpkin
5. stepladder
6. rowboat
7. horse
8. elephant
9. whale
10. Statue of Liberty

VALUABLE INTRODUCTIONS (page 18)
OCTOPUS
DECADE
TRIATHLON
UNICYCLE
SEPTET
NONAGENARIAN
BIKINI
HEXAPOD
QUADRUPLETS
PENTAGON

LOST IN THE WOODS (page 19)

SCRAMBLED PICTURE (pages 20-21)

DIGIT DOES IT (pages 22-23)
Dear Inspector Digit,
I may have dropped the Hopeless Diamonds and struck out, but you will never tag me before I reach home. If you don't take any short stops, you may find twenty diamonds before I make my way to the next safe!
R.B. Ives

HIDE AND GO SEEK (page 24)
Harvey is hiding at spot #9. This is the only space not in anyone's direct line of sight.

TIME OUT (page 26)
Wrong items:
The two is a different type.
The three is backward.
Five is tilted.
Seven and eight are reversed.
Ten is in a Roman numeral.
The hour hand is pointing to twelve, but the minute hand is pointing between 4 and 5.
There are only four minutes marked off between the five and six; six minutes are marked between the ten and eleven.

NUMBER RECALL (page 26)
1. 5
2. 9
3. 11
4. 18
5. 8
6. 1
7. 4
8. 20

SHAPE SHIFTER (page 27)

SAND ART (page 28)

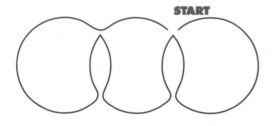

START

PLAYING FOR POINTS (page 29)

Thirty-five points had been scored. Bill had eight, Kim had five, Frank and Carol each had six, and Chad had ten.

TRAINING GROUND (pages 30-31)

A. Six cars
B. 720 feet
C. 120 feet per minute
D. In real life, the track would measure 54,720 feet, or just under 11 miles.
E. 38 feet

Toughie: It takes two seconds for the train to pass completely through the tunnel. It takes one second for the front to appear from the mouth of the tunnel and another second before the end of the train gets to that point.

MATHMAGIC (page 32)

The trick is to subtract 250 from whatever number you are given. Then drop the last two digits.
The numbers that are left will give you the month and the day of the person's birth.

COLOR BY NUMBERS (page 33)

MYSTERIOUS MAP (pages 34-35)

Ted:	Max's Grocery
Ed:	Ike's Bikes
Fred:	Polly's Pet Shop
Jed:	Ann's House

FISH STICKS (page 36)

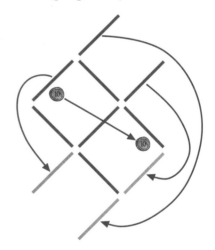

BOAT BUILDER (page 37)

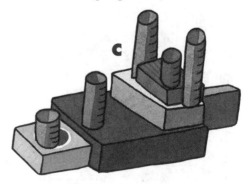

C